Henry M. Prentiss, Bruce Rogers

The Great Polar Current

Polar papers old and new

Henry M. Prentiss, Bruce Rogers

The Great Polar Current
Polar papers old and new

ISBN/EAN: 9783337331719

Printed in Europe, USA, Canada, Australia, Japan

Cover: Foto ©Andreas Hilbeck / pixelio.de

More available books at **www.hansebooks.com**

THE
GREAT POLAR CURRENT

POLAR PAPERS
OLD AND NEW

BY

HENRY MELLEN PRENTISS

CAMBRIDGE
Printed at the Riverside Press
1897

TO JAMES GORDON BENNETT

WHOSE

JEANNETTE EXPEDITION

DEFINED THE FIRST FIVE HUNDRED

MILES OF THE POLAR CURRENT AND OPENED

THE WAY FOR THE NANSEN DRIFT AND

FOR THE FINAL SOLUTION

OF THE ARCTIC

QUESTION

CONTENTS

INTRODUCTION

READING lately an article on the scientific results of Nansen's voyage, in the February number of the Nineteenth Century ("Recent Science," III.), by Prince Kropotkin, in which he states that Nansen's expedition was suggested largely by the drift of the Jeannette and of the Jeannette relics, I was reminded of a paper I had sent to the New York Herald in 1883 on the scientific results of the Jeannette expedition — which was never published — and of other papers written during the search for the Jeannette in the fall of 1881; and I was somewhat surprised to find how persistently I had argued for the great polar current, even in my letter to Markham and in that which the Herald published, both of which were written before the Jeannette was heard from; while in my paper on the "Results" I had proposed this very Arctic voyage on the identical plan that Nansen adopted, and had even given a fair general description of the Fram so many years before she was built.

At the same time it is interesting to find how nearly Nansen's drift agrees with my forecast, and how completely it has proved my theory of the depth, the currents, and the general hydrography of the polar basin, — a theory about which most of the leading Arctic experts, both of England and America, have been, to say the least, exceedingly skeptical.

I have never seen, in the whole voluminous mass of Jeannette literature, any satisfactory *résumé* of the scientific results of the voyage, — a voyage which was popularly regarded as a failure, because

De Long did not reach the Pole, did not even attain a high latitude, and especially on account of its tragic ending. Yet Prince Kropotkin gives the Jeannette voyage its true place in Arctic history when he speaks of Nansen's drift as " embodying the drift of the Jeannette and the East Greenland ice-drift in one mighty current." . . .

" A formidable ice-current, almost as mighty, and of the same length, as the Gulf Stream, . . . a current having the same dominating influence in the life of our globe, has thus been proved to exist."

This great Arctic current, of which the connecting link has been discovered by Nansen, having its inception north of Bering Strait and Wrangell Land, flows northwesterly above the New Siberian Islands, and northerly across, around, or very near the Pole, or at least far to the north of Franz Josef Land, and thence southerly by Spitzbergen, by the east coast of Greenland, by Labrador and by Newfoundland, until it meets the Gulf Stream, — its influence being felt even as far as Cape Cod on the coast of New England. Thus it flows across some seventy degrees of latitude, and is about 5000 miles long.

BANGOR, MAINE, May 1, 1897.

THE JEANNETTE SEARCH AND THE
POLAR CURRENT

BANGOR, MAINE, November 27, 1881.

CLEMENTS R. MARKHAM,[1] ESQ., C. B.,
Sec'y Royal Geographical Society.
DEAR SIR, — I am unknown and without experience in Arctic matters, and therefore feel that I am taking a liberty when I address you on the subject. My only excuse is that, having of late thoroughly read up on the Arctic, I have come to a conclusion as to the probable course and present position of the Jeannette, differing considerably from any I have yet seen. I also wish to urge an

[1] Now Sir Clements Markham, K. C. B., F. R. S., F. S. A., President of the Royal Geographical Society. This letter was never published. See Appendix, Markham's letter.

English naval search expedition to Franz
Josef Land, and to consider the situation
from an American point of view. The
Jeannette Expedition is lost in " the
unknown region." For the second time
there is to be a great " Franklin search,"
but with this difference. Franklin sailed
under Admiralty instructions on a special
line of exploration, and consequently the
search was confined to a comparatively
small portion of the Arctic area. Captain De Long, however, was at liberty
to go where he pleased. The Jeannette
was not a government vessel, although
officered and manned from our navy, and
De Long was, therefore, free to incur
extra hazardous risks of losing her ; and
from his known views and plans, often
expressed, we are quite sure that he was
determined to go to the Pole in any way
he could get there, and if the coast of
Wrangell Land did not continue far to

the north, to take to the pack, to penetrate the ice-field as far as possible, and
then alternately to steam and to drift, or
if necessary to drift with wind and current, hoping to be carried across the Pole
and out between Spitzbergen and Greenland, with or without his ship. He is one
of the most venturesome men that ever
went into the Arctic; especially when we
consider the present state of our knowledge of the formidable character of the
polar ice. Even in view of the daring attempts of English explorers, we can only
say that he is the least hampered man or
the most reckless. This attempt to float
across the Pole may well be compared
with Stanley's rash attempt to float down
the Congo, except that Stanley knew that
the river must bring him to the ocean,
while unfortunately De Long may come
out, if at all, on any one meridian of the
360.

Consequently, there are 360 possible theories as to the course of the Jeannette, of which, since the last reports of the Rodgers, I would suggest the following as the most plausible. The Jeannette was last seen by a whaler, September 2, 1879, about fifty miles south of Herald Island, steering north for that island. Probably the sea was too rough there for De Long to land, as Captain Berry of the Rodgers found it, at times, this summer; and as Captain Berry has landed there twice, and Captain Hooper of the Corwin once, this year, and as the island has been thoroughly searched and no cairn found there, it is quite certain that De Long was not able to land. Then he may have gone on to the north and west and found Wrangell Land to be an island; probably there was such an ice pack along its shores, possibly also stormy weather, that he did not find it practicable to land

there. He would not be turned away
from his main object for the sake of exploring an island no larger than one of
the New Siberian Islands, especially so
late in the season, with plenty of open
water as far as he could see to the north
and west. Proceeding north, he would
come to the pack, very likely about where
the Rodgers did this year, and would explore its edge, and make efforts to penetrate it in various places at points one
hundred and fifty to two hundred miles
north and northwest of Wrangell Land,
and find it practically impenetrable —
the sea growing deeper as he went north,
no prospect of any land very near toward
the north, and no current moving northward or otherwise. The season of 1879
was probably an open season in those
waters, about the same as this year, and
his experience, and his track to the north
of Wrangell Land, about the same as that

of Captain Berry last summer. Very
likely De Long would not run the risk of
getting beset in that position, because,
finding no current to the north, and know-
ing from Baron Nordenskjöld's experience at his winter quarters at Serdze the
preceding winter, and from many other
sources, that the prevailing fall and
winter winds in that whole region were
from the north and northwest,[1] he would
naturally fear being drifted to the southeast and east into a region where he could
not expect to make new discoveries or

[1] De Long did not meet Nordenskjöld, and the prevailing winds on the Siberian coast several hundred
miles to the southward were mostly of continental ori-
gin, and so were no criterion, as it proved, for the
winds north of Wrangell Land. From all the data
then possessed — from what was known, supposed, or
reported — as to the force and direction of the winds
on the north and west sides of Bering Sea, and also of
the winds at the New Siberian Islands and at Franz
Josef Land, I theorized that the region of equal winds
should be placed farther west towards the New Siberian Islands; later I learned that De Long found the
"doldrums" nearer to Wrangell Land. See page 65.

any brilliant progress. Consequently, I believe he abandoned that meridian and went westerly, probably north of Wrangell Land, as, if he had gone south of it, he could probably have landed and built cairns, while the ice or a gale may have prevented his landing on the northern side. Captain Berry carefully examined the coast of Wrangell Land all the way around, and found no cairns, or traces of the Jeannette; and yet De Long would undoubtedly have landed, for various strong reasons, if it had not been very inconvenient to do so, or if it would not have involved too great a loss of time, when he had not a day to lose. As to cairns, however, he never intended that search should be made for him where he went in to the Arctic, if he did not find Wrangell Land to extend far to the north. Captain Berry did not find the ice-conditions favorable for crossing to the west on the north side of the island, and had no great object to gain by trying to push through the ice in that direction. Yet, the ice may have been more open when De Long was there.

After passing Wrangell Land, I think that De Long may have steered for the New Siberian Islands, in the hope of getting into a region where the prevailing winds would be more favorable to his project, or at least where they would not be against him; also to explore the Russian polynias, with the expectation of finding a current running to the north or northwest, around to the northward of Franz Josef Land and out by Spitzbergen. Perhaps he did not find the polynias so extensive as he hoped, and, trying the ice everywhere, may have had to follow the shore by Cape Chelagskoi, and so on to near the mouth of the Lena, where a Yakut reported that he saw a three-masted steamer, or the smoke of a steamer, September 13, 1879. The New York Herald was not inclined to credit this report, on account of the short time between the 2d and the 13th of September. Yet De Long may have made rapid progress; the winds may have favored him. He evidently did not waste much time at Herald and Wrangell islands. Nordenskjöld and Palander often covered greater distances in shorter periods in their northeast passage. The Yakut may have been incorrect about the date, and probably could not fix it exactly; but such a report was not likely to arrive without some foundation, and the Jeannette was the only possible foundation for it. Finally, Nordenskjöld and Lieutenant Hovgaard believe the report, and certainly no one is more competent to judge of its credibility.[1]

[1] There was a similar unfounded report from the same region about Nansen last winter.

Thence from off the mouth of the Lena De Long may have steered north late in September to the New Siberian Islands, built cairns there and deposited records. He may have wintered there, but that would be no object to him. For if there were any open water to the north, and there probably always is in that locality in September, he would certainly go as far as possible to the north of those is- lands, then penetrate the pack in the most favorable place he could find, and keep on through it till he was finally beset or frozen up.

If, therefore, we may suppose him fast in the pack in October, several hundred miles north of the New Siberian Islands, which way would he drift? No one can say. We possess no specific data from which to form an opinion. The whole hydrographic, geographic, and meteoro- logical mystery of this unknown region

is involved in this question. But my
theory is, and De Long's theory was, that
the Siberian ice and the drift-wood of the
great Siberian rivers are carried across the
Pole, or in the vicinity of the Pole, north
of Franz Josef Land, and out in the extensive and never-ceasing ice-drift between
Spitzbergen and Greenland. Otherwise,
where does all that ice come from? The
Russian polynias may not be so extensive
or so constant as many have supposed, but
all admit that there are large areas of open
water and of loose ice there every year,
and possibly all the year round, — the ice
always drifting away to the north, perhaps about as fast as it freezes. From
what little we know of the ice about the
New Siberian Islands, we judge it is not
very heavy away from the land. It may
have time to grow old and thick before it
gets across to Spitzbergen; but that the
great mass of that ice-stream, nearly two

hundred miles wide at Spitzbergen, comes from a wide and probably deep polar sea north of Siberia and north of Franz Josef Land seems as clear to me as it did to Stanley that the Lualaba was the Congo and ran to the ocean. No doubt there is a north end to Greenland, though perhaps not at Cape Britannia, and some of the ice of the "paleocrystic sea" may get out and come down the East Greenland current; yet if the whole of it came out there, the ice of that sea would not be so old and heavy, say forty to one hundred feet in thickness. Then very little such heavy ice is found in the East Greenland current — the ice there not averaging over one quarter to one half the thickness of that off the mouth of the Mackenzie River, Banks' Land, Prince Patrick's Island, the head of Smith's Sound and north end of Greenland, though it is much heavier than the ice of Baffin's Bay

and of the straits and sounds discharging
into it.   There is a large body of land in
the Antarctic covered by a thick glacier
that extends far out into deep water all
around its coasts, and ice forms in winter
on the deep sea, for hundreds of miles to
the north, all around the outside of the
glacier ice-cliff, often drifting away and
gradually spreading out in ever extending
circles from the central land ; yet it must
often be many years before it melts, as
Sir James C. Ross found the ice about as
thick as that which comes out between
Spitzbergen and Greenland, — though one
year he succeeded in penetrating eight
hundred miles of this ice, because it was
so loose he could generally sail through it.
In the Arctic, however, the polar area is
surrounded by continents, and the ice has
practically only one opening of consequence in which to float out to the southward to be melted.   No ice of any amount

gets out through Bering Strait, — certainly very little that could be called polar ice. There is a constant flow of ice out of Baffin's Bay, but it consists almost entirely of one-year-old ice, formed in the bay itself and in the various sounds and straits opening into it. The polar ice is packed at the heads of all those straits, in tremendous jams of floes so large and thick that but few of them are needed to block a strait twenty miles wide ; and Arctic explorers are agreed that only a small portion of that polar ice gets through Barrows Strait, the channels between the Parry Islands, Wellington Channel, Jones' Sound, or Smith's Sound. The ice between the Spitzbergen-Franz Josef Land group and Nova Zembla does not drift out far to the south, or it is ice mostly found on the parts of the Barents Sea where it originates. The currents run in, rather than out, to the north of Nova Zembla, and

although there may be an eastward drift
along the southerly coasts of Franz Josef
Land, it is not likely that much ice comes
out that way from the polar basin to the
eastward and northward of Franz Josef
Land. Probably there are lands north
of the American continent — perhaps a
chain of not very large islands — extending westerly from the meridian of Greenland and of Smith's Sound, as suggested
in the Threshold of the Unknown Region,
which prevent the great mass of the ice
in the inclosed area from drifting across
the polar sea, or from getting out into the
East Greenland current; so that much of
that ice, imprisoned by such islands —
partly it may be by prevailing winds driving down to the heads of narrow channels
and against the coast — goes on for many
years increasing in thickness before it gets
away to more southern latitudes where it
will melt. The discovery that Wrangell

Land is an island, and not a prolongation
of Greenland, does not disprove this theory, nor seriously affect it; for even if
there is a larger opening than we supposed into this paleocrystic sea, the ice
cannot get out there, because there is no
current out. On the contrary, the prevailing winds keep the ice from floating out
in that direction. The fact that the ice
in terrible southerly gales, long continued,
does not blow away from these American
and island coasts more than a few miles
tends to prove such an inclosure of this
sea as practically to keep the ice from
floating out of it. While on the other
hand, the ice off the Siberian coasts, outside the shore ice, does float away to the
north, which indicates that there is sea,
and not land, in that direction, — a sea
that probably extends through to Greenland. The fact that there is a deep sea
north of Spitzbergen — deepening the

farther you go north — helps this theory.
For if the polar sea were entirely inclosed
by land, the ice would accumulate faster
than it would melt, and the whole sea,
however deep, would be covered with ice
so thick that it would be akin to a floating
glacier, melting only at the edges near the
warmer land and at mouths of rivers on
its southern coasts.   That such is not the
case is mostly due to the outflow at the
Spitzbergen-Greenland opening.   Consequently, this ice in the Greenland current
is but five to twenty feet thick, much of
it only one year old, which tends to show
that the ice in this supposed sea, extending from Siberia north of Franz Josef
Land, and probably at the Pole itself,
is no thicker, and that it may possibly,
to some extent, be navigable, — although
perhaps not to a 400-ton, 100 horse-power
steamer, like the Jeannette.   The Baffin's
Bay one-year ice was not fairly naviga-

ble to sailing vessels. They were often crushed by it and constantly beset. Even a small steamer like the Fox cannot always get through it, but it is navigable to steamers like the Alert, Discovery, Proteus, Pandora (Jeannette), and the whaler Arctic. Such steamers cannot navigate this Spitzbergen or polar ice, at least with any more safety and certainty than the small sailing vessels of 50 and 100 tons of the earlier explorers could sail through the middle-pack of Baffin's Bay.

I would like to see a steamer of 10,000 tons and 10,000 horse-power, built on the best model that could be devised for resisting ice pressure, with a bow armed to split the floes, and formed so as to rise upon them and crush them, of the greatest possible strength consistent with coal-carrying capacity, with sufficient power to force the great floes apart and to squeeze through between them, commanded by

Captain Markham, with Captain Adams of the Arctic to assist him. Such a ship, possibly, could contend with Spitzbergen ice, and steam in between Franz Josef Land and Nova Zembla, around Franz Josef Land and to the Pole, and out by Spitzbergen.[1] She would sail in deep seas, would not draw much more water than the ice, and if there were as many polar stations and expeditions all around the Arctic Circle as there will be a year from now, to retreat to in case of accident, to a corps of expert seal and bear hunters such a trip might not be extra hazardous.

Leaving speculation aside, the practical work for England is to send an expedition to Franz Josef Land. The only thorough search for the Jeannette is a search of the whole border of the unknown area. De Long is within it somewhere,

[1] It is now evident that no conceivable ship could make such a holiday excursion.

and we do not know where he will come out. If he comes out at all, it is highly probable that he will leave his ship behind, crushed or permanently grounded in a stranded ice-pack; or he may drift hopelessly about till his provisions are exhausted. There should be a complete search. The Rodgers will remain about Bering Sea. A sledge expedition, starting from where the party are now landed, near Cape Serdze (?), with Colonel Gilder (who was with Schwatka), will probably search the Siberian coast as far west as the mouth of the Kolyma, repeating Wrangell's longest journey in the reverse direction. Lieutenant Ray, U. S. A., of the Signal Service Corps, has established his meteorological station for three years at Point Barrow, and will secure communication with the Esquimaux, as far east as the mouth of the Mackenzie River. He will certainly make a search expedition in that direction this winter or next, as he can command the services of a whole Esquimaux tribe, and is prepared for such a journey. There was a rumor of shipwrecked men on that coast, which was not credited, because it was too vague from want of an interpreter, and because none of the Esquimaux at Point Barrow had heard of it, — a very unlikely thing, even if it had any foundation. It is thought that the old Indian (?) was trying to tell of the whaler Vigilant, with dead men aboard, that drifted on to the Siberian coast. Still Lieutenant Ray will undoubtedly investigate the rumor and examine that coast. Then, another reason why he will do it is that the Bering Sea whalers and the San Francisco geographers all believe that it was impossible for the Jeannette to penetrate far into the ice north of Wrangell Land, — that stopped the Rodgers. But they have no doubt that

De Long tried it, and that the winter winds would drift him, beset in the pack, to the south and east.

Accordingly the present talk in America is of sending an expedition to Melville Island, to search the shores of Banks' Land, Prince Patrick's Island, etc., and the New York Herald urges England to send an expedition down the Mackenzie River to search easterly to Banks' and Wollaston Lands. Yet, I do not see how such a party could help De Long much, even if they should find him, and question that policy, especially if it should take the place of an English search to Franz Josef Land. But this would be a good opportunity to try again the Northwest Passage, by the way of Peel, Sir James Ross, and Simpson's straits, with a good steam whaler chartered for the purpose, with the philanthropic motive of assisting in the search in addition to the glory of making the passage. Such a ship should be prepared to winter, and if caught halfway, to form one of the international circle of meteorological stations round the Arctic, and thus to fill a gap that it would be very desirable to have occupied. Besides, the party should have sledges and Esquimaux hunters, as they might have to abandon their ship. The Proteus has landed Lieutenant Greely at Lady Franklin Bay, where the Discovery wintered in 1875-76. Thus another meteorological station, for three years, has been established. Lieutenant Greely proposes to join in the search by sledging to Cape Joseph Henry. He is well prepared for exploration. Dr. Pavy will probably determine, at last, whether Cape Britannia is the northern point of Greenland, and Greely may possibly cross Grinnell Land to the west from the head of Lady Franklin Bay, and continue the search and exploration on its western coast. His steam launch may be very convenient for laying out depots for the Cape Joseph Henry and Greenland trips. Living thus through several summers, he may be able to accomplish some surveying that the English expedition did not have time or opportunity for, especially if he has some fresh men sent him every year, as planned. Commander Cheyne also proposes to go to the same place, to try his experiments with balloons. His projects are here regarded as visionary. His journey to the Pole over the ice does not promise great results, and balloon journeys are too uncertain, even in an inhabited country in the temperate zone. He is lecturing in New York to raise enthusiasm in support of his project, probably supposing that if we were rash enough to support Mr. Bennett and Captain De Long in a daring undertaking, we might even assist his im-

practical expedition. When our government consented to the Jeannette Expedition, it was presumed that Wrangell
Land was of continental size, or at least
that there was a shore running far to the
north, or a series of islands that could
be followed far into the unexplored area.
If De Long had found such a shore, he
would have followed it as far as possible,
and would have come back the same way,
with or without his ship. Our searches
in the Corwin, last year and this, and
the Rodgers search, were based on that
theory, and all these proposed searches on
the north coast of this continent and about
its northern extensions and islands would
have been much more important if Wrangell Land had extended to the north, as
Captain De Long was last seen going up
the easterly side, and if beset, would surely have drifted easterly. The Rodgers
search, then, would have followed up that

coast-line. Since the last report from the Rodgers, showing that this theory was wrong, the most hopeful field seems to be to the west, instead of to the east. But, to continue round the circle, there will undoubtedly be one of the international meteorological stations established at Spitzbergen next year, and it is to be hoped they will try to reach Gillis Land, or the west coast of Franz Joseph Land, with sledges. It will be a most important field, with reference to the possible relief of the Jeannette party, and the same can be said, with less emphasis, perhaps, of the proposed similar station at Jan Mayen, and of the proposed station at Nova Zembla; but the Russian station at the New Siberian Islands is very important with reference to the Jeannette search. The Russians may discover cairns of De Long, and if he has not drifted so far as he hoped, these islands may be his line of retreat — to the mouth of the Lena. The proposed trip of Lieutenant Hovgaard, of the Danish navy, to Cape Chelyuskin, and perhaps as far east as the Lena, completes the circle. Probably Lieutenant Hovgaard places too much reliance on the Samoyede report of the two corpses, and the bottle or barrel of whiskey near the mouth of the Yenisei, as it is certainly possible that walrus hunters or adventurous traders may have followed the track of Siberiakoff's vessels to that point. The Jeannette went into the Arctic on total abstinence principles, — little if any whiskey among her stores. So that report is capable of an explanation without regard to the Yakut report of the steamer seen off the mouth of the Lena.

Of course, an effectual search at the edge of the pack for the Jeannette party, drifting on the ice, will be made everywhere, by hundreds of whalers, walrus hunters, and sealers that frequent the Arctic seas. Commander Wadleigh did good work this year at St. John's, N. F., Iceland, Hammerfest, and on his Spitzbergen cruise, in warning all the world to be on the lookout for such a party on the ice, or for such a ship beset in the ice, informing them of the possibility of their coming out this way, and giving them pictures of the Jeannette. Those vessels are much more likely to pick up De Long, if he ever gets out to frequented waters, than any search expedition. Indeed, those who thought that the Jeannette might get out this year by Lancaster Sound now think that Captain Adams, of the whaler Arctic, made the most important search of the season in his brilliant voyage up Wellington Channel, Barrows Strait, and down Peel Sound. If Sir James C. Ross had had such a season and such a ship as the Arctic, in 1848, he might possibly have found Franklin's ship, and also Crozier, at the time he returned from Back's River and before he started on that last terrible wandering to reach his old Esquimaux friends at Igloolik.

So the circle of next year's Jeannette search is complete, all but Franz Josef Land, which is left for England. The reasons why England should make such a search are overwhelming.

First, it offers the best chance of success and is unprovided for, and England has always taken the lead in philanthropic enterprises.

Second, England owes it to America to take part in the search. We sent four expeditions in search of Franklin or of the Franklin records, — De Haven, Kane, Hall, and Schwatka. Hall spent five years looking for possible survivors among the Esquimaux of Repulse Bay, Boothia, Regent's Inlet, and Igloolik, and for the journals of the voyage, and it is extremely probable that some of them did survive for a year or two, and may have reached Igloolik. At any rate, Hall's search had a fair basis of probability. Schwatka tried what Sir Allen Young, in the Pandora, failed to accomplish, — a summer search for the records at King William's Land, when the snow was off the ground, — and made a most remarkable sledge journey with only a month's supplies for a year's trip, and lived by hunting, — a course that would not be so safe in higher latitudes. Again, Stanley found Livingstone, provided him with supplies for further explorations, and relieved the very great anxiety of England.

Third, it is due to Mr. Leigh Smith that England should see what has become of him. He has illustrated England in Arctic exploration more than any other man since the expedition of 1875. Still,

I believe he got to Franz Josef Land this year, probably late in the season, and that he is safe, as he has provisions for wintering. He is in a position to relieve the Jeannette crew, if they get where he is; but I suppose he is not prepared for extended sledge journeys to search for them, and possibly the Willem Barents crew are there somewhere, needing assistance — at least, I have not heard of their return home.

Fourth, England is almost the only nation that has not agreed to establish an Arctic meteorological station for simultaneous scientific and weather observations. This should not be. Franz Josef Land is just the place where one is most needed to complete the line. There is only one in a very high latitude, the Lady Franklin Bay station (Spitzbergen is uncertain), and Franz Josef Land is most important of all. England has a splendid meteorological service, and surely no nation is so largely interested in the laws of storms as affecting commerce. Leigh Smith, Captain Markham, and the Willem Barents have shown the way to be perfectly sure and safe to good steamers in ordinary seasons, and the former has even selected a good place and sure harbor for the station — Eira Harbor.

Fifth, all English Arctic authorities agree that Franz Josef Land offers the widest and most interesting field for geographical and scientific exploration of any in the Arctic — with also the best chance of carrying the exploration to a very high latitude.

There are numerous other general reasons why England should — and officially too — keep on in her preëminent course of Arctic exploration. Even a generous rivalry with other nations, in such a work as this, is no mean motive. The United

States has had six Arctic expeditions, of one kind and another, this year, and has now four government expeditions wintering in the Arctic, all doing valuable work, and one running terrible risks, in the advancement of the world's knowledge — and has only begun the business. England has plenty of competent and some experienced naval officers who are anxious to be employed in this service, and I suppose the Alert and Discovery are still good ships for this work. It would not be overdoing it if she should send a fleet to Eira Harbor, with coal transports in addition, and annual supply ships to recruit the crews and carry the mails. One ship could go up the east coast of Wilczek Land, more especially to search for the Jeannette; another up the west coast of Zichy Land, the line of exploration most generally recommended by English Arctic authorities; and another up Austria

Sound, which would probably reach the highest latitude of all, and perhaps find the Jeannette aground on the north shore of Petermann Land, — by a sledge expedition, — and rescue De Long's party from certain death.

Why should not Austria Sound be as navigable as Smith's Sound? Payer found smooth ice there generally, — one-year ice, — and large spaces of open water on his return journey, as early as May. His report gives us considerable reason to conclude that it can be navigated even as far as Cape Vienna in August or September. It is true that Leigh Smith found the entrance closed in 1880, but he did not seriously attempt to get through then, as he was not prepared to risk being caught for the winter. Probably there is a current or a strong tide up the sound, and those entrances may be blocked with ice-jams; but the ice is not very heavy,

the season may be more favorable, and
the Alert could perhaps ram her way
through.

I would make only one more suggestion.
Is it not generally agreed now that Esquimaux fare — fresh meat and Arctic meat
— is the most sure preventive of scurvy?
McClure had no scurvy at Banks' Land
and got plenty of game. The Franklin
search sledge expeditions, too, usually
got plenty of game. Hall lived for years
on walrus, seal, reindeer, etc. There are
plenty of walrus at Franz Josef Land in
summer, and bears winter and summer.
If there are bears, there must be seals.
All that saved Weyprecht and Payer
from scurvy and enabled Payer to make
such an extended sledge journey was the
skill of his Tyrolean hunters in killing
bears. Joe and Hans saved the lives of
the Polaris party in their winter drift
on the floe by their skill in hunting seals.

If Franklin had had a good corps of hunt-ers, the lives of the whole expedition might have been saved, the scurvy, of which they possibly died, would have been prevented, and they might have lived with or like the Esquimaux, until they got out to where they would have been rescued.

Very truly yours,

HENRY M. PRENTISS.

THE JEANNETTE

New York, December 14, 1881.

To the Editor of the Herald.[1]

According to the Earl of Ellesmere, the naval intimates of McClure said of him when he sailed for the Arctic by the way of Bering Strait to search for Sir John Franklin : " That man will not return by the way he has gone, unless at least he shall meet with Franklin or find reasons connected with his rescue for retracing his course ; he will return eastward, or he will return no more." Commander De Long's friends might have said of him when he sailed in the Jeannette : " That

[1] This letter was written on the train from Boston to New York, and was published in the *New York Herald* December 17, 1881, five days before the news came from the Jeannette, December 22.

man will not return by the way he has
gone, unless at least he should find the
easterly coast of Wrangell Land extending far to the north ; he will return across
the Pole and by the Atlantic, or he will
return no more."

THE JEANNETTE'S COURSE

Captain Berry has now shown Wrangell Land to be an island, and that its
coast failed him. Consequently De Long's
friends now believe that he took to the
pack, to penetrate it as far as possible,
and if permanently beset to drift with it
across the Pole.   There are two principal
theories as to De Long's course.   The one
generally accepted by the Bering Strait
whalers and by the San Francisco geographers is that when De Long met the
polar pack, perhaps where Berry found
it, one hundred and fifty to two hundred
miles north of Wrangell Land, he en-

tered the pack there and made his way
in the ice as far as possible to the northward, and when beset or frozen in drifted
with it, and if he got free again in 1880
still fought his way northward till again
beset. They also believe that the prevailing winds north of Wrangell Land
are from the west and north, that there is
an easterly current, and that De Long is
drifting toward the east; that, therefore,
the search should be made on the northern coasts of America and of Greenland.

But my theory is that De Long went
to the westward; that he tried the pack,
as Captain Berry did, north of Wrangell
Land, penetrating short distances here
and there, and finding the ice very formidable. There being no prospect of penetrating it very far, and no favoring current being discovered, he probably then
turned to the westward, hoping to find the

Russian polynias and to get further to the
north on the meridian of the New Siberian Islands.   He may not have been
able to proceed directly across to the
west, and may have followed the coast till
near the mouth of the Lena before turn-
ing northward again.   This would be the
surest course to take to reach the New
Siberian Islands.

ACROSS THE POLE

I believe that De Long would prefer to
make the attempt on the meridian of the
Lena, because he knew that the prevailing
winds at Franz Josef Land are easterly,
as observed by Payer and Weyprecht,
and that a great current brings down the
polar ice between Spitzbergen and Greenland in a constant stream, two to three
hundred miles wide, winter and summer.
There is great probability that there is
a regular ice-drift from the region of the

New Siberian Islands, caused by prevailing winds and currents, through a deep sea north of Franz Josef Land, across or near the Pole, and out to the south between Spitzbergen and Greenland. Hedenstrom, Anjou, and Wrangell have shown that there are large open seas north of Siberia, or at least that the ice drifts away far to the north of the New Siberian Islands in summer and fall. Therefore the presumption is that there are no islands or lands to the north, while on the other hand Collinson, McClure, Sherard Osborn, McClintock, and Nares have shown that the ice in long-continued and violent southerly gales never drifts away more than a few miles from the shore on the North American and Greenland coasts, from Point Barrow to Cape Britannia. Consequently they reason that there are sufficient undiscovered islands or lands to the north of this continent to stop the main body of this ice from drifting away across the polar basin. They call this the " paleocrystic sea " — where the ice averages from forty to one hundred feet in thickness, grounds in ten or twelve fathoms of water, and is often a century old.

LAND-LOCKED POLAR ICE

Very little of the ice of this sea gets through the many narrow channels leading to Baffin's Bay ; and as but a trifling quantity of this thick ice is found in the East Greenland current, it is to be supposed that Greenland extends beyond Cape Britannia, or that there are islands or shoals to the north to block the way. The fact that Wrangell Land is not a continent does not disprove the theory of the paleocrystic sea, as the prevailing winds would prevent the ice from drifting out to the westward by Wrangell

Land, even if there are not unknown
islands to the northward of Point Barrow
to block up the passage.

FREE POLAR ICE

The Spitzbergen and East Greenland
ice is not like the paleocrystic; it is only
from five to twenty feet thick, not a fifth
part as heavy on the average; much of
it, even far to the north of Spitzbergen,
being only one-year ice, very little of it
can come from a paleocrystic sea. It
must come from the centre of the polar
area, from north of Franz Josef Land and
from north of Siberia. I do not believe
that the immense amount of drift-wood
with which the northern shores of Spitzbergen are lined and covered can be sat-
isfactorily accounted for in any other way
than by supposing that it comes from the
mouth of the Lena, around by the north
of Franz Josef Land.

THE NORTHWEST COURSE

I believe De Long preferred the northwest course, rather than the northeast,
from Wrangell Land, and hoped to come
out by Spitzbergen, rather than by the
northerly point of Greenland. Hence
I think the coasts of Franz Josef Land,
Siberia, Nova Zembla, and Spitzbergen
the most hopeful lines of search for the
Jeannette party. Still, there is an ab-
solute uncertainty as to the course Lieutenant De Long took, and possibly he
did not know that the prevailing fall and
winter winds north of Wrangell Land
were from the north and west. Baron
Nordenskjöld came out of Bering Strait
before De Long went in, and did not meet
him. Consequently, De Long may not
have known that Nordenskjöld observed
almost constant northerly and westerly
gales at Cape Serdze Kamen the whole

preceding fall and winter. As nearly all the whalers caught in the ice in the northern part of Bering Sea have always drifted away into the unexplored region, and as the ice in that sea drifts far to the north in southerly gales, De Long may have thought the position two hundred miles north of Wrangell Land as good a place to start from as any for his daring voyage, or drift, across the Pole.

THE EASTERLY DRIFT

If De Long went in there, we may almost say we know, since Nordenskjöld's observations, that he must have drifted to the eastward rather than to the westward; then the most important field of search is on the northern coasts of this continent, and this brings us to the question of the Northwest Passage. There are three sound reasons now for trying the Northwest Passage : —

First, and much the most important, the search for the Jeannette.

Second, the advantage of having an international polar station, even for only one winter, halfway between our Point Barrow and Lady Franklin Bay stations, if the expedition did not succeed in making the whole passage the first year.

Third, the glory of making the passage, as it has never been made by a ship.

THE SEARCH

As to the search, it is necessary. For the second time in the history of polar research, an expedition is probably lost in the Arctic. There is to be another great Franklin search, with this difference: that was an English and American search of a limited segment of the polar circle; this will be a universal search of the whole border of the unknown region, participated in by nearly all the civilized nations of the earth. The whole Siberian coast will probably be searched by Captain Berry, Nordenskjöld, Lieutenant Hovgaard, and the Russians. The Russian international polar station at the mouth of the Lena, or at the New Siberian Islands, will be very important, for I believe De Long built cairns and left notice of his progress there, if he was not prevented from landing by heavy weather or ice, as he was at Wrangell and Herald islands. Spitzbergen and Nova Zembla will be international stations, and England will search Franz Josef Land, I hope, on all its coasts and sounds with a large government expedition for the Jeannette and for Leigh Smith. I think this the best chance for rescuing the Jeannette party. England is the only important nation that has not agreed to form an international polar station, and it is to be hoped, now that she goes to Franz Josef Land, she will go there to stay, as there is no other such promising field for scientific and geographical research. All the international polar stations will be Jeannette search stations as well, and will send out sledge expeditions.

WHALERS TO THE RESCUE

Five hundred whalers, walrus hunters, and sealers will search for the Jeannette at the edge of the pack in all the seas that they frequent, from the Kara Sea to Spitzbergen and East Greenland, up Lancaster Sound, and in Bering Sea. The Herald and Captain Wadleigh, in his last summer cruise in the Alliance, have interested the whole Arctic business world in the search. There remains the northern coast of this continent. Lieutenant Ray, at Point Barrow, will probably be able to search halfway to the mouth of the Mackenzie River, and Lieutenant Greely, at Lady Franklin Bay, will probably go northwest to Cape Joseph Henry, and will find out whether Cape Britannia is the termination of Greenland. But there is a tremendous gap between Greely and Ray. There ought to be three expeditions to fill it: one to make the Northwest Passage, one to Melville and Prince Patrick islands, and one up Jones Sound to search the west coasts of Ellesmere, Grinnell, and Grant Lands.

THE MACKENZIE RIVER

The proposed Hudson Bay Company search is desirable, but it is not sufficient. Such expeditions cannot carry extra provisions to relieve a starving crew, or, if they do, they cannot get very far. A hundred miles either way from the mouth of the Mackenzie is about all they would accomplish, if they were to carry extra provisions of any consequence. What is needed is a ship loaded with provisions, like the Rodgers. Then, as to the international polar stations. It is possible, if a ship attempts the passage and does not find the Jeannette party, and returns, that she may have to winter somewhere between Dolphin and Union Strait and Bellot Strait. If so, the party could make all the simultaneous meteorological and scientific observations made at the other stations. There are to be eight or ten such stations all around the Arctic next winter, and the establishment of these winter stations is especially important to our American Signal Service.

THE NORTHWEST PASSAGE

It is generally agreed by all Arctic authorities that the Northwest Passage can be made by such a ship as the Jeannette, or the Rodgers, by way of Peel Sound, Sir James Ross, Dease and Simp-

son straits, following the coast-line everywhere, and navigating the coast water.
Sir Allen Young and Mr. MacGahan of
the Herald, thought of trying it when
they went in the Pandora (Jeannette) to
make the summer search for the Franklin
records at King William Land; but they
were not prepared to winter, found the
season unfavorable, and turned back when
near Bellot Strait. Captain Adams, of
the whaler Arctic, thought he could have
made the passage this year. He went further down Franklin Strait than any ship
ever went before, except Franklin's ships,
and then was not stopped by ice, but by
the interests of his owners. It might be
difficult or impossible to navigate the Victoria Strait, where Franklin's ships were
stopped, because, from northwest winds
and tides down McClintock Channel, and
slack water caused by the meeting of the
Baffin's Bay and western tides, that strait

has always been found packed full of paleocrystic ice. But the great body of warm fresh water poured down by Back's Great Fish River tends to keep open Sir James Ross and Simpson straits, and thus to make the passage possible. When we consider what Collinson, McClure, and Franklin accomplished, navigating these narrow and crooked channels obstructed with numerous rocks and shoals, and with strong tides, in sailing vessels, it seems almost certain that a powerful steamer could make the passage, and probably in one season, if so fortunate as to have one like that of 1881.

WORK FOR THE RODGERS

I propose, if no one else wants to try the passage, that Captain Berry, with the Rodgers,[1] should attempt to come home

---

[1] The Rodgers was burned in winter quarters at St. Lawrence Bay.

that way next August. He will pick up
his Siberian sledge party by that time.
He can safely leave Bering Sea and Point
Barrow to the whalers and to Lieutenant
Ray. If he has to winter, your corre-
spondent, Colonel Gilder, is familiar with
the only questionable part of the Northwest Passage, and if worst came to worst,
could show them how to live like Esquimaux, and guide them out to Hudson's
Bay. There is nothing better for Captain
Berry to do. He will not run the risk
of losing a government expedition, trying
to discover unknown lands to the north
of Bering Sea. This is the best line of
search left him after his sledge party's
return.

A UNITED EFFORT

There is a great awakening of interest
in Arctic matters, and there is to be a
grand assault made next year on all the

Arctic mysteries, — meteorological, hydrographical, geographical, and scientific,
— a very complete and thorough Jeannette search, and the wide space between
Ray and Greeley ought to be effectually
filled by a searching ship starting from
Bering Sea.

H. M. PRENTISS.

THE RESULTS OF THE JEANNETTE EXPEDITION [1]

To the Editor of the Herald.

In 1879, the Wrangell Land route to the far north was considered one of the most important that was left to be explored. From the information obtained by Wrangell, the discoveries of Kellet, of John Rodgers, and of various whaling captains, and according to the theories of such eminent Arctic authorities as Clements Markham and Dr. Petermann, Wrangell Land was generally supposed to be a large mass of land stretching far to the north, — perhaps even to the Pole itself, — and Dr. Petermann believed it

[1] Never published. See Appendix, Letter from the *Herald*.

to be the other end of Greenland prolonged across the Pole. The very slight
rise and fall of the tides, the accumulation of ancient stratified ice of extraor-
dinary thickness, indicated that the sea
north of America was mostly inclosed, —
a sort of Arctic Mediterranean. All other
routes, except that by Franz Josef Land,
had been abandoned as impracticable.

De Long undoubtedly planned to follow the coast of Wrangell Land as far
north as possible with his ship, to find a
harbor and winter there, to make advance
depots of provisions that fall, and to follow the coast with sledges in the spring.
He would make all the scientific observations, explore a large part of the unknown region, and attain a high latitude.
It was the general belief of people best
acquainted with the subject that he would
accomplish all this, and all the geographical societies were anxious to see some-

body make the attempt.   De Long hoped
to reach the Pole, but that was more than
good judges expected.

The Jeannette, however, was caught in
the pack and drifted across the Wrangell
Land of the maps, — across where the
Blevin Mountains were laid down; and it
was discovered that the fabled Wrangell
Land of the last fifty years was merely
an ordinary island of small importance.
The theories of geographers had to be
readjusted, and this route of Arctic exploration was proved to be a geographical
illusion.   The subsequent exploration of
the island and of the seas for one hundred and fifty miles farther north by the
Rodgers Search Expedition was a most
fortunate and valuable supplement to De
Long's discovery, for which Lieutenant
Berry is entitled to the highest credit;
yet the important disclosure that Wrangell Land was an island and an impracti-

cable base for higher exploration belongs
to De Long, and would have been published to the world if the Rodgers had
never sailed in search of the Jeannette.

Consequently, it is now settled that
there is no coast left by which any
further very great advance can be made
into the unexplored region except in the
Franz Josef archipelago, — another step
towards the solution of the great Arctic
problem.

THE GREAT POLAR CURRENT

The Jeannette drifted in the ice nearly
two years, and thus established the existence of an Arctic drift or current. There
is no reasonable doubt that the ice regu-
larly drifts from the northwest of Wrangell Land in about the same general direction as the course of the Jeannette, as indicated on Lieutenant Danenhower's chart.
There may be variations in different years,

but there is probably a moderately regular annual drift in the general direction, whether caused by a current or by the preponderance of the prevailing winds. This movement was so constant and direct in the spring of 1881, and so powerful in May and June along to the east and northeast of the New Siberian Islands, that it is beyond doubt that the ice from the region to the northwest of Wrangell Land floats off to the north and west, and consequently to the Atlantic, to be melted in more southern latitudes. It does not drift out through Bering Strait. It cannot forever stay in the polar basin, for if that sea were entirely inclosed on the line of the Arctic Circle, it would be filled with ice to the depth of one or two thousand feet, if not everywhere to the bottom, — an enormous glacier, a polar ice-cap! For the mean annual temperature is so low in the polar regions that not half the annual accumulation of ice and snow could ever be melted in those latitudes. At 75° or 80° ice freezes in still water to seven or eight feet in thickness, while in summer three or four feet of the surface of the pack melts away; but at the Pole and within the 80th parallel — a circle of fourteen hundred miles in diameter — more ice must freeze, and less can be melted.

The polar sea, however, — over large areas, — is so deep, and has such gyrating and conflicting currents, that the ice never becomes absolutely fixed over its whole surface, and there is no doubt at all that the great mass of the polar ice drifts out of the Arctic Ocean through the deep and broad opening between Spitzbergen and Greenland into the Atlantic, in a constant and regular stream, — the discharge of an incipient glacier.

Lieutenant Danenhower graphically

characterizes the region north of Wrangell Land, where the Jeannette drifted for more than a year in a complicated series of rhomboids and circles, as the "Arctic doldrums," — a locality where there is no current, or merely slight currents in the nature of eddies, and no prevailing winds.

From the east of Wrangell Land the drift is probably north and east, and is obstructed by islands to the north of America and to the north of Greenland, so that some of that ice may be a century in getting out by the north point of Greenland into the Atlantic; and this accumulates by crushing into masses and by the excess of the annual freezing and snow-fall over the annual melting, until it becomes fifty to one hundred feet thick. No relic of any of the whaling ships, nor of whole fleets of whalers, frozen in or beset in Bering Sea and drifted away northerly into the unknown region, has ever again been seen, while on the other side of the Arctic Ocean the driftwood of the Lena River is piled up in heaps on the shores of Spitzbergen.

The Jeannette drift indicates that the ice from the northwest of Wrangell Land floats off to the north of Franz Josef Land and joins the great East Greenland current. The large mass of fresh water from the Lena, Yana, Kolyma, Olenek, and other Siberian rivers — especially in the summer — must give a considerable impetus towards the beginning of a current, and must assist the movement of the ice out by the New Siberian Islands, across by the way of the Pole, or at least to the north of Franz Josef Land.

This drift of the Jeannette destroys some theories as to Arctic currents that have met with wide acceptance among the hydrographers. Sir Wyville Thomp-

son thought that the Gulf Stream ran
into the Arctic by the north end of Nova
Zembla along the coasts of Russia, Siberia,
and North America, and by the northerly
point of Greenland, — thus making a cir-
cuit of the polar sea, — and joined the
great East Greenland current out into
the Atlantic.   But the drift of the Tegethoff by Nova Zembla northeasterly, and
around to the north and west in a semi-
circle to Franz Josef Land, discredited
that theory, and this Jeannette drift gives
it a final quietus.

Thus the course of the Jeannette drift
throws new light upon the obscure question of Arctic currents.   In addition, it
suggests a possibility of

A NEW SCHEME OF POLAR EXPLORATION

A ship might drift in the ice — or upon
the ice — from the New Siberian Islands
to the north of Franz Josef Land, and

possibly far to the north and near or across the Pole, and out into the Atlantic between Spitzbergen and Greenland.

Much has been learned of Arctic hydrography by the involuntary movements of ships beset in the pack. The abandoned H. M. S. Resolute drifted from Barrows Strait to Labrador, and this drift of the Resolute, together with that of McClintock in the Fox, of De Haven with the first Grinnell Expedition, and of the Polaris party on the ice floe, determined the currents out of Lancaster and Smith's sounds through Baffin's Bay and Davis Strait to Labrador and Newfoundland. The drift of the Hansa was a striking proof of the East Greenland current. The wonderful drift of the Tegethoff — from Nova Zembla far to the northeast, and around and back and finally to Franz Josef Land — demolished some hydrographic theories and showed the great and increasing depth of the polar sea the farther the vessel was borne towards its centre. Thus involuntarily Franz Josef Land was discovered; and though the expedition was a miserable failure as to its main object — the Northeast Passage — and though Payer and Weyprecht left their ship behind on top of a grounded ice-floe, yet the expedition was otherwise a grand success and made the most brilliant Arctic discovery of this generation.

. If the Jeannette had been forced up by the pressure on to a solid floe, like the Tegethoff, she might possibly have been drifted out by Spitzbergen in another year or two, might have got clear of the ice the second or third year, before rounding Cape Farewell, and might perhaps have sailed back to New York safe and sound, thus making the tour of the world by a new route, — across the Pole. Again, if De Long had gone into camp

for the season on the largest and heaviest
floe he could find after the Jeannette was
crushed, he might have drifted out in one
year to the vicinity of Spitzbergen. Then,
dragging his boats to open water, he would
probably have found walrus hunters, or
even some search expedition, at Spitzbergen.

For a long time before she was crushed
the Jeannette had been drifting at the
rate of twelve miles a day, and there is
every reason to suppose that those ice-
fields keep on at that rate across the polar
basin all summer; but twelve geographical miles a day would have covered the
distance of fourteen hundred miles in four
months, and De Long's ice-floes would
have passed by Spitzbergen before the
next winter. It is absolutely possible
that a ship could drift in the ice from the
New Siberian Islands to opposite Spitzbergen between June and October. But

a winter drift might be quite different. Then Siberia is in a state of congelation, and all its rivers are at their lowest stage. In the deep seas of the polar basin, the pack, though always in motion, is frozen up and to a certain degree consolidated, and no intelligent prediction can be made, at present, of what the winter drift would be. Most likely it would prove to be very inconstant and irregular.

AN IDEAL POLAR SHIP

No doubt it was very hazardous for De Long to put the Jeannette into that twenty-foot ice and to run the risk of getting beset. He had a perfect right to take the risk, — that was a part of the original plan, — and the ship did not belong to the navy. The whalers, sealers, and walrus hunters take just such risks every year. No practicable ship could be devised that would endure the direct

maximum pressure of the polar ice ; such
ice must go under her and lift her out of
water, or must go through her side. No
ship, however, has yet been built solely
for the purpose of polar exploration, except the Eira. The whalers and sealers
must have large carrying capacity. Other
Arctic ships have been selected somewhat
at random.

Possibly a ship could be modeled
mainly with reference to escaping the
pressure ; of such a shape that the ice
would naturally run under her, with a
rudder and screw that could be unshipped
and lifted out of water, with no protrud-
ing keel, forefoot, or stern-post, or with
a rudder-post that could be raised with
the rudder, so that there would be nothing
to prevent the ice from running under
the ship and nothing to be injured or carried away, — the strongest possible ship,
with all kinds of composite sheathing, an

outer skin partly covered with steel plates, and an inner skin and layers of felting with another sheathing inside the felting; with many compartments, braces, trusses, and bulkheads; with a solid bow and large steam power, to ram the floes so as to force them apart, — built mainly for strength, coal-capacity, steam-power, and to rise to pressure.

Very likely, when firmly frozen in during the winter, the ship could not rise to pressure, but no Arctic exploring ship that has yet drifted, beset, through the Arctic night has ever been crushed in the winter. The summer is the dangerous time, when the floes are more broken and the ship gets free.

With such a ship, a man like De Long might proceed to the New Siberian Islands by either way, from Bering Strait by Cape Chelagskoi, or from the North Cape by Cape Chelyuskin, and get as far

north as possible in September, for all
Arctic waters are less encumbered by ice
in August and September, and then he
might deliberately put his ship into the
ice and ram her through the polar pack
until she was finally beset and frozen in,
to drift with the winds and the currents —
whither? I believe he would drift to the
Atlantic. He should be so equipped as
to be able to live on the largest and thickest floe in his vicinity all winter, if he
should lose his ship, and he should have
all kinds of boats provided for all possible
emergencies. And thus, in any case, he
would have a fighting chance of getting
out alive, to give the world the benefit of
his discoveries.

In this random ice-voyage he might
discover new lands ; he would sound and
record the depth of the sea ; he might
dredge a new submarine fauna, — perhaps the surviving remnant of a past geo-

logical age, — and he would be a living proof of the polar drift, and should give many new data to the meteorologists and to the hydrographers.

De Long contemplated the chance of an involuntary drift when he started. If Wrangell Land should fail him, he had determined to put his ship into the pack, and, if caught, to see where he would drift and what he would discover. He hoped to drift across the Pole to the Atlantic.

DE LONG DISCOVERED NEW LANDS

The Jeannette, Henrietta, and Bennett islands are a northeasterly extension of the New Siberian group. De Long's most important work, however, was in exploring new seas. Von Wrangell's Siberian " polynia " is a myth.

In all their tremendous dog - sledge northerly journeys over the Siberian seas,

Von Wrangell, Hedonstrom, and Anjou always came to open water. They never failed to find the sea free from ice late in the summer as far as they could see from the Liakhoff Islands. Petermann, Kane, Hayes, and many others, based their (exploded) theory of " the Open Polar Sea " very largely on these polynias of the Russians. Now De Long has abolished the polynias from our Arctic maps, and he would easily agree with Nares, with Payer, and with everybody else, at the present day, that there is no " Open Polar Sea; " that is, at least, not in the winter. In August that sea is open along the shore all around. The ice-pack grounds, in many places, in thirty or sixty feet of water. This " land-water " freezes every winter and melts in summer. The ice is melted away from wide areas, or driven off by the currents, opposite the mouths of all the rivers; but the ice-fields themselves drift away to the north from Bering Sea, and generally from the Siberian coast. The polynia opposite the Lena does not wholly depend upon the warmth of the Lena water, but largely upon the enormous quantity of water poured out by the summer flood, and upon the drift to the northward that is caused by the surplus of waters of all those Siberian rivers.

It was very unfortunate for De Long that more was not known of the local distribution of the tribes along the Siberian coast. He should have steered his boats for the mouth of the Yana or for Upper Bulun. Melville has detailed the geography of all that region, — another valuable result of the Jeannette Expedition. Many and painful have been the sacrifices while man has been slowly acquiring his present knowledge of his planet, and there have been none more heartrending than the tragedy of the Lena. Still future generations will honor the promoter of the Jeannette Expedition for his philanthropic liberality, and De Long will have everlasting fame for his daring enterprise and heroic martyrdom in a noble cause. The world will never rest content until the earth is fully explored, nor until all its phenomena attainable to human science shall be known and utilized.

HENRY M. PRENTISS.

BANGOR, ME., November 6, 1883.

THE NORTH POLE AND THE SOUTH POLE [1]

AT the North Pole, the Arctic Ocean is probably a thousand fathoms deep, while the South Pole is at the centre of a glaciated table-land thousands of feet above the level of the sea. The Arctic Ocean discharges its ice in fields, some of of it a century old, and a hundred feet thick, mostly by an ocean current through the narrow gap between Spitzbergen and Greenland ; while the Antarctic ice floats off, in the form of great tabular icebergs hundreds of feet high, one or two thousand feet thick, and often miles in area, in all directions, as along the spokes of a wheel, from the ice cliffs encircling the

[1] Published in the *Overland Monthly*, July, 1890.

whole glaciated surface of the Antarctic continent.   The South Pole will be finally attained by a sledge expedition, across seven hundred miles of inland ice; while the only way to reach the North Pole is to float across it.

The more we know of the earth, the smaller it seems, and we shall inevitably explore every hole and corner of it.   If one may judge by what has been accomplished since Columbus set sail from Palos, another century should complete the work.   Three quarters of the world was then unknown; yes, nine tenths of it was to Europeans an unexplored region: while now, since Stanley has filled the last important gap in the map of Africa, less than one sixtieth part of the earth's surface remains to be explored.

The men who plant a scientific observatory at the South Pole, and there maintain it for three years, will win undying fame. It may cost millions of money, the work of a thousand men, the loss of a hundred lives, but money is a drug in the markets of the world, and human life is cheap; and neither the men nor the money will be found wanting.

We have been blindly groping in the Arctic darkness for a century past, hunting for a Northwest Passage; for Sir John Franklin; for the Open Polar Sea. Parry even sought in one of his four Arctic voyages to reach the Pole itself, by a boat expedition through and over the floating ice north of Spitzbergen, but found that he was traveling against the stream. Disraeli ordered Nares to go to the North Pole, and Nares followed the coast-lines of Smith Sound, discovered by Kane, Hayes, and Hall; and when the land ended, Markham failed in his attempt to reach the Pole over the floating ice of the Arctic Ocean.

De Long started for the Pole by way
of Bering Strait, to follow the coast-
line of Wrangell Land, which was as-
sumed by Petermann to be the westerly
end of Greenland prolonged across the
Pole, and by Clements Markham to be
the southerly end of an extensive Arctic
land. But finding Wrangell Land to be
only a small island, De Long allowed his
ship to be frozen in, as he had boldly
decided to keep on to the northward,
and, if necessary, to float in the pack to
destruction, or to new discoveries.

Many of the most important Arctic
discoveries have been made by such involuntary drifting. The Resolute, the
Fox, and above all the Polaris party on
the ice floe, determined the currents of
Lancaster and Smith sounds, of Baffin's
Bay and of Davis Strait, to Labrador
and Newfoundland; and the drift of the
Hansa proved the East Greenland cur-

rent. Payer drifted a year and a half in
the Tegethoff, and discovered Franz Josef
Land, and from his drift we can infer
that the opening between Franz Josef
Land and Cape Chelyuskin is mostly
closed by lands or islands. De Long's
drift began in what Danenhower graphically termed the "Arctic doldrums,"
north of Wrangell Land, where, frozen
into the pack, he floated about at the
mercy of every wind, backward and forward, round and round, for a year before
he got fairly started; then he was carried
by the ice in a northwesterly course five
hundred miles toward the Atlantic, and
discovered three islands; but his ship was
crushed at a point northeast of the New
Siberian Islands. The Jeannette had
been drifting fast in a direct course for
months before she sank, and if she had
not been wrecked she would have drifted
in another year to the north of Franz

Josef Land, and out between Spitzbergen
and Greenland into the Atlantic. Dr.
Nansen says that the articles abandoned
on the ice by De Long, picked up three
years after off the coast of Greenland and
carried to Denmark, are of such a character as to establish their own identity.
The driftwood on the north coast of
Spitzbergen comes mostly from the Lena
River. The ice of the polar sea would
become a glacier if it were not brought
out to warmer latitudes by some ocean
current, and undoubtedly the great body
of the polar ice does come out between
Greenland and Spitzbergen.

The polar ice north of Bering Sea
drifts northeasterly around the north
point of Greenland, northwesterly north
of Franz Josef Land, and northerly
across the Pole, and then out into the
Atlantic.

The polar sea is two thousand miles in

diameter. Though comparatively shallow north of the continents, it is over eight thousand feet deep north of Spitzbergen, and grows deeper towards the north. It is always covered by fields of ice; the ice constantly accumulates; it freezes not only through the six months' night of winter, but more or less all the year round. The ice is never stationary; fields crush against fields, floes against floes; they pile up at the edges, and over-ride and under-run each other. That part of the sea north of America and west of Grinnell Land is probably inclosed to some extent by islands, or possibly northwesterly winds are prevalent, and drive the ice down against all those island coasts, from Banks' Land and the Parry Islands to the north end of Green-land, so that some of the ice gets to be a century old, partially stratified, and a hundred feet thick, before it ever gets

out to the Atlantic to be melted. All the
Franklin search expeditions found such
ice on those northwestern shores. Captain Nares called it the "paleocrystic
ice." All the narrow channels flowing
towards Baffin's Bay are choked up with
it, and that is the reason why no ship
could ever get through any of them. The
Kara Sea also is an Arctic eddy, in which
much of the ice is very old and thick.

The principal advantage to be gained
by drifting across the North Pole would
be to determine the hydrography of the
polar ocean. Even if there were an
island at the Pole, no regular scientific
station could ever be maintained there.
A ship might drift there, and even winter there, and the party might get out
alive in boats by way of Spitzbergen, but
no regular communication could with certainty be kept up with a station on such
an island.

The coasts of the islands of the Franz
Josef group, and probably of other islands
and lands not yet discovered, of Jones'
Sound, and the west coast of Grinnell
Land, the northeast coast and north end
of Greenland, will eventually be explored,
and the geography, the amount of land
and water, the depth and the currents of
the polar sea, and all other Arctic questions of interest to science, will be in-
vestigated.   Another expedition, larger
than Dr. Nansen's, should cross Greenland
in its widest part, from Sabine Island
to Upernavik, or from Scoresby Sound
to Disco.

The Northwest Passage can now be
made in any favorable season by some
Arctic yachtsman and sportsman like
Leigh Smith in the Eira, just for the sake
of sport, for glory, and incidentally for
science, by avoiding the channel where
Franklin was beset and taking the back

channel around the east side of King
William's Island, and by Dease and
Simpson Strait, following the land-water.
Still, such an expedition should be prepared to winter on the way; and, in case
of disaster, to come out overland with
hunters and magazine rifles, perhaps to
Hudson's Bay, in the track of Schwatka
and Gilder.

The one important Arctic expedition
of the future, however, will follow Nordenskjöld by Cape Chelyuskin, or more
likely will follow his track backward from
Bering Strait by Cape Chelagskoi, to the
open water at the mouth of the Yana and
of the Lena; push north the same year, or
the next, in September, when that sea is
most open, to the region northeast, *and
as far northeast as possible, of Bennett
Island*, where the Jeannette sank; proceed north until beset, and then drift in
the pack across or near the Pole to the

Atlantic. The ship may run aground on Franz Josef Land, or may be crushed, or may be forced up on top of the ice as the Tegethoff was, and so may float to the Atlantic before the ice melts from under her. No hollow ship can endure the direct crushing force of the paleo-crystic ice; but a ship might be designed of the greatest practicable strength and solidity, of such shape that when nipped the ice would tend to run under the ship and lift her entirely out of water. If the ship were crushed, the crew could probably escape over the ice, and with boats. Parry, Kane, the Hansa crew, Payer, Leigh Smith, the Proteus and Polaris parties, and numerous others, have made such voyages out of the Arctic with boats, or by floating out on the ice-floes. No exploring expedition that has tried it, or that was not disabled by scurvy, ever failed to succeed in such an attempt.

Franklin was not properly equipped; he waited too long, and, instead of trying to go back by boat the way he had come, planned a land route south across British America. Greely succeeded, but he did not find the support he had a right to expect at the mouth of Smith Sound. De Long had inconceivably bad luck: he had to start against the current; his boats were too heavy; too much time was lost in various ways, so that he was too late in the season; he met a furious gale, which swamped one of his boats, and partially disabled the crews of the two others; while his own boat's crew was the unluckiest of all, in missing the natives. If De Long had known all we now know of the Lena Delta, he would have been saved. If he had floated all summer, and wintered on the largest and thickest floe he could find near where his ship went down, he would have had a fair

chance of escaping safely by way of Spitzbergen.

The Antarctic, however, is by far the
most important field of future polar exploration.

First, a steamer should circumnavigate
the Antarctic continent. Sir James Ross
sailed round it; but as the Erebus and
Terror were sailing ships, he could not
always closely follow the coast. Besides,
his principal object was to make a magnetic survey, and to locate the southern
magnetic pole. But no steamer has ever
been to the Antarctic continent. All
attempts at Antarctic explorations ceased
over forty years ago. Probably no harbor could be found where a ship could
winter; hardly a spot has ever been
found where a boat could land. Ross
landed once at the risk of his life, on a
narrow ledge at the foot of an ice cliff;

D'Urville landed in a bay surrounded by cliffs of glacier ice; Wilkes and the United States Exploring Expedition never found a chance to land; and Weddell, who sailed into the Antarctic south of the Atlantic, never reached the land.

Ross sailed along an ice cliff two hundred feet high, in water two thousand feet deep, for four hundred miles. That was fifty years ago, before anything was known of the glacial period. He knew nothing of glaciated continents; he could hardly call it land; so he named that cliff the " Great Icy Barrier." At the height of the great ice age, a ship might have sailed for a thousand miles along such a cliff, a hundred or more miles out from the American coast, from off Cape Cod to Newfoundland and Labrador; or along the European coast from a hundred miles off Ireland to the North Cape. If the ice should ever entirely melt from the

Antarctic continent, it might not all prove to be solid land. The European ice-sheet once spread out smoothly from the Scandinavian highlands over the Gulf of Bothnia and the Baltic, Denmark, the German Ocean, and the British Isles, and far out to sea. The extensive ice cliff that Ross discovered proves the existence of a far more extensive land, as the ice cliff in a deep sea off Great Britain in the glacial period must have indicated the continent of Europe.

At the foot of the volcanoes Erebus and Terror, at the west end of Ross's Great Icy Barrier, there were still no harbors, as all the bays were filled with glaciers. The glacier not only comes to the sea level, but runs far out to sea, all around the Antarctic continent, at least as far as is known; still some place will undoubtedly be found in that more than five thousand miles of coast, where a party can be landed with coal, supplies, and materials to build and maintain a permanent station, from which sledge expeditions can go over the inland ice to the South Pole. Dr. Nansen has shown that such traveling is practicable, by crossing Greenland, three hundred miles, two years ago, over such inland ice.

A scientific station at the South Pole could be established and maintained for several years for half the money that was spent in the search for Franklin. A thousand men, relays, and a progressive system of stations, with annual supply ships, — the expedition should be on some such scale to insure a perfect success. For all this sledging, Scandinavian hunters, equipped like Doctor Nansen's Greenland party, would seem far more suitable than the English sailors, who often made sledge journeys of a thousand miles in the Franklin search.

For a preliminary survey, any good steam whaler could probably pass through the loosely packed ice to the Antarctic coast, steam around the South Pole in one season, and find a landing place suitable for a station. Open water would be found along an ice cliff for most of the way in January, February, and March. The Arctic Ocean is crammed full of ice; it is jammed against the shores, the narrow openings out of that sea (all but Bering Strait) are choked with it as it is carried out by currents toward the Atlantic, and navigation along Arctic coasts is correspondingly difficult. But as there is nothing to prevent the ice from radiating off the coasts of the Antarctic continent, very little obstruction would be met. There would be many icebergs to be avoided, but the daylight would be almost continuous. The winds or currents might carry the ice against the land on some coasts, but it would be mostly ice that was only a year or so old.

A party might land somewhere and make a dash for the interior; but nothing very important can be done in the way of inland exploration, without a large force of men, plenty of time, and a permanent station.

What is the advantage to be gained?

Many chapters have been written on the advantages of polar exploration, but there is room for only a few suggestions.

The southern hemisphere is ten degrees colder than the northern; how cold is it at the South Pole, if in the centre of a high tableland on a glaciated continent? To understand the past history of the earth, we must know all about glaciated continents. We have only two of them left, and the Antarctic is more important than Greenland, for it is larger, colder, and more completely glaciated.

The glacial period still exists to-day in the Antarctic, in as severe a form as ever in Northern America or in Northern Europe.

We are just beginning to make a scientific study of the weather. We can never perfect that science, however, even if the world should unite in an international service, until we learn all about the weather conditions of the polar regions. We have learned much of that unknown force called electricity, and are beginning to suspect that this globe is a great electrical machine with magnetic poles of positive and negative electricity, and that all planets and suns must be electrified, and even that gravitation may be the result of electric attraction. When Franklin caught the lightning with his kite, the world may well have said, "Very curious, but what is the good of it?" Discoveries that to our ignorance seem unimportant often lead to great results. The questions relating to the southern magnetic pole are some of the most important that scientists would like to investigate in the polar regions. The whole civilized world could well afford to contribute to a great scientific Antarctic exploration.

I SENT the preceding paper to Dr. Nansen several months before it was published in the " Overland," and he penciled an interrogation point at the end of the opening sentence, "At the North Pole the Arctic Ocean is probably a thousand fathoms deep." The opinions of experts in Arctic matters have generally favored the conception of shallow seas throughout the Arctic area, because the sea had always been found shallow north of the continents as far as soundings had been taken. Yet the great oceanic depression occupied by the Atlantic was known to continue northward west of Spitzbergen, and the most northerly sounding showed a depth of over 8000 feet about 150 miles north of Spitzbergen, while now Nansen has extended the Atlantic basin far towards the centre of the polar area and across some 1400 miles, nearly to the New Siberian Islands, with soundings of 10000 to 12000 feet.

Now, although Prince Kropotkin admits that 2000 fathoms 300 miles from the Pole indicates an equal depth at the Pole and far beyond it, he says the 3000 fathoms line passes within a hundred miles from Boston, and suggests that the great ice-current in which the Fram drifted may run in a deep trough, or downward fold of the earth's crust, some 300 miles wide, along the north side of a submarine oceanic ridge, of which Spitzbergen and Franz Josef Land are the visible projections, and which may extend far to the eastward towards Siberia, and that the sea may grow shallow again the other side of this comparatively narrow depression, thus rendering possible the existence of land about the Pole.

It has seemed to me, however, that the form of the polar basin and its broad connection with the Atlantic, as well as the general slope of the continental masses about it, naturally indicated that its greatest depth would be somewhere near its centre. The gentle inclination towards the north of British America and of Siberia would naturally continue for a long distance under the polar sea, as the soundings show. De Long found only a few hundred feet of water the whole length of his drift from Wrangell Land to the New Siberian Islands; Berry found about 500 feet at his farthest, north of Bering Strait; but the sea deepens rapidly north of Point Barrow and towards the mouth of the Mackenzie, soundings of 800 feet and over having been taken all along within 100 miles of that coast.

Scientific opinion now favors the theory of the general geological permanency of continental masses and of oceanic basins; that when the planet first cooled, there were large areas of depression and of elevation, such as we now see on the moon; and although the continental masses and the comparatively shallow surrounding seas, and the ocean floors as well, have had intermittent periods of local elevation and depression, that nevertheless the earth has on the whole, in a broad and general way, maintained its original form, and the great oceanic hollows have always remained; the decadent continents always encroaching upon the sea around their borders, but never trespassing very seriously on the distant ocean depths.

So when Nansen finds the shallow Siberian sea rapidly changing to a fathomless ocean — and is obliged to improvise a new sounding apparatus — at a point about 400 miles north of the Siberian coast, it is like Prince Kropotkin, on his way home from Boston, sailing off from the shallow seas over the submarine moraines left by the inland ice of the glacial period — George's Bank, Stellwagen's Bank, the Grand Banks — and across the 3000 fathoms line of the Atlantic.

As the Asiatic continental mass ends some 300 miles off the north coast, analogy would indicate a similar result on the other side of the " Arctic gulf," all the conditions being similar, and thus we should find a deep ocean, and no more islands, at an equal distance north of the Parry Islands and before getting halfway to the Pole, a third part of the way north of Point Barrow.

But if the Pole is somewhere near the centre of an ancient and permanent oceanic depression, no land would be likely to exist there. If the region were volcanic, there might be volcanic islands, as in the South Seas. The neighboring lands, however, as far as we know them, are not volcanic; at least there are no active volcanoes nearer than Iceland.

Yet the theory I have held for many years as to the depth of the polar sea and as to the absence of land there was largely based upon the Arctic ice conditions, upon the character of the ice in the current west of Spitzbergen, upon the very existence of such a current, and upon the fact that it has no polar icebergs.

If the extensive polar basin is mostly of oceanic depth, there must be an oceanic circulation, as is indicated by Nansen's deep-sea temperatures, and much Gulf Stream water must pass into it, partly perhaps between some easterly extension of the Franz Josef group — far beyond Payer's discoveries — and Cape Chelyuskin; but probably most of the Atlantic

water goes up along the west side of Spitzbergen and spreads out over the bottom
of the polar basin as an under-current.
The discharge of the Siberian and American rivers is an important element in the
matter of Arctic currents, and cannot be
neglected, but is entirely inadequate to
account for the immense body of water
that flows out of the Arctic seas.

Sir Clements Markham said last November : —

" Personally, as I do not believe in any
land near the Pole, or on this side of it
beyond Franz Josef Land, I trust an attempt hereafter will be made to explore
another portion of the Arctic regions.   I
believe there is land, probably in the form
of large islands, between Prince Patrick
Land and the New Siberia Islands."

That is a broad gap to fill.   I do not
believe in much land north of Bering
Strait, for the ice drifts away freely far

to the north in prolonged southerly gales, and analogy would suggest the prolongation of the Atlantic basin towards the Pacific at Bering Strait, and the deep water north of Point Barrow points in the same direction. But in these previous papers I have repeatedly suggested sufficient reasons for expecting to find more or less land north of America.

Therefore I think favorably of the project of exploration to the north, westward from Jones' Sound.

The nearest continental extension towards the Pole, as far as appears, is at the north end of Greenland; but Admiral Markham found the sea grow deeper as he went north over the floe-ice, and Nares reported to Disraeli that the Pole was impracticable from that base of attack. I think that Greely would agree with Nares, although very likely there are still other islands beyond Cape Washington.

Nansen tried for the Pole, of course, and got halfway to it, setting a mark, in something less than a century since Parry's farthest, that it may take another century to surpass. He went three and one half degrees further north than Parry, two and five sixths degrees further north than Markham and Lockwood, and got within three and three fourths degrees, or within 226 geographical miles, of the Pole, — almost as near to it as from New York to Washington. If we accept Kropotkin's dictum, however, that there is a region of some 1400 miles by 1000 that we know less about than any such extensive region on the planet Mars, then adventurous men will try to get there, and nothing can prevent them. There seems to be something magnetic about the North Pole — an idea, cultivated by a century of heroic endeavor, that even drove a romantic world-ruler like Disraeli to give formal instructions to a naval officer to go and hoist the British flag upon it. If men must try for it again, the only way to get there, previous to the invention of a practicable flying-machine, is to drift there in an Arctic ship like the Fram. As for Mr. Andrée, he should make a few trial thirty-day balloon voyages about the centre of some large inhabited continent, before trying his first great experiment in such an unfavorable locality as Spitzbergen.

Nansen was frozen in some 260 miles west of where the Jeannette was crushed, although nearly 100 miles further to the north (still he was then to some slight extent under the lee of the northern extension — that De Long had discovered — of the New Siberian group), and the Jeannette, even if she had not sunk, might not have drifted north of the point where the Fram was beset. But if Nan-

sen could have attained a point two or
three hundred miles to the northeast of
the place where the Fram was beset, or
could have crossed through the ice-current to a point "as far northeast as possible of Bennett Island," he would probably have had a better chance of drifting across the Pole. It might be found
impracticable to go up the east side of
the New Siberian Islands, the eastern
coasts of which group are probably always
blocked by the ice-stream driving against
them from the eastward; but as these
islands stand in the way of the ice-current, the seas in their lee are left open
after the ice of the previous winter is
out of the way; and Nansen may know,
or may not know, whether he could have
got further to the northeast across the
current if he had been on hand earlier in
the season to try the ice everywhere in
that direction. Indeed, from De Long's

experience it seems hardly probable that Nansen could have crossed the stream of heavy floe-ice, after passing to the west of Bennett Island, that De Long's party traveled over on their retreat; for although Sverdrup worked the Fram across the current through the pack for 180 miles above Spitzbergen, this feat was possible only because the pack begins to open up and spread out in that vicinity.

Nansen's voyage might be repeated several times without any nearer approach to the Pole.

Captain Berry had a more open season in 1881 than De Long in 1879, and reached a position 150 miles north and east of where the Jeannette was frozen in; and it is very likely that, being further away from continental influences and further away from Wrangell Land, a ship might drift nearer the Pole, starting from Berry's farthest point, than the

Jeannette would have drifted; still, as far as we can judge it would take five or six years to get across, and it would be mostly luck whether the ship drifted across the Pole or passed by at some distance on either side.

But there is no longer any pressing need of going to the North Pole, for Nansen has probably discovered about all there is to be discovered in that part of the Arctic. The result of any further attempt, very likely, would not justify the expense and probable waste of human life and energy; for all the salient features of the north polar basin are now known, and Nansen has just given us the key to the whole Arctic mystery, — just as when Stanley arrived at the mouth of the Congo there was nothing left to do in the exploration of Africa but detail work.

March 13, 1897.

NANSEN'S scheme, his ship, his drift, as well as his sledge-journey over the moving ice, are each and all perfectly unique in Arctic annals, — a new departure in polar exploration; and each and all are so supremely successful that others may rush in, with a light heart, to follow in his footsteps, expecting that on a second trial they might drift nearer the Pole, or another dash might be made for the Pole with dog-sledges.

It is very doubtful whether a better start could be made from the New Siberian Islands. The Fram was frozen in, September 25th, at the edge of the pack

[1] Since sending the preceding paper to the printer, Nansen's book, *Farthest North*, has been issued.

at the most northerly point of the open
water, about 280 miles north of the mouth
of the Lena; and after drifting northwesterly a few days over a sea that was
nearly a mile in depth, the ship then
floated southeasterly, in about five weeks,
over 100 miles to a position 100 miles
west of Bennett Island. But the sea had
been growing shallow for the last fort-
night, until on November 9th the depth
was only fifty-seven feet, which indicates
a very near approach to the New Siberian archipelago. Thence the drift was
almost directly north for the next 100
miles, into water over two miles deep.
Dr. Nansen does not express any opinion
as to whether a better position could be
reached for entering the pack, as he was
too late in the season to do much exploring, but I think he would agree with me
that the chances are against a fairer start;
and besides, another time he might get

frozen in earlier in the season and much farther south, just as the Jeannette was frozen in three weeks earlier than the Fram, and very far south of the latitude attained by Berry, in Bering Sea.

A ship starting from the same region would be likely to drift over much the same course, with no more chance of veering to the north than to the south of the track of the Fram; and as to the dash to the Pole, Nansen thought if he had had the dogs from the Olenek he could have got much farther, but it seems quite evident that if he had got very much farther he would have fared far worse, for the polar pack is better traveling in March and April than in the summer months. Besides, a man should have Nansen's experience, and in fact be Nansen, to dare such things; and although he only beat the Fram eighteen miles in the race for the Pole, still I am glad that Nansen made the venture. That plan of spending the winter at Franz Josef Land with nothing but cartridges was sublime; but I hope nobody else will try it and arrive too late in the season.

This trip to the Pole over the ice is very enticing. Dr. Pavy wanted to try it (over again) from Cape Joseph Henry, Peary from Greenland. No one will start from Franz Josef Land, because the drift will be against him, but others may try it from some later-to-be-discovered lands north of the Parry Islands. I don't believe Esquimaux could do it with dogs, — I don't believe polar bears could do it; for game is scarce inside the eighty-sixth degree, probably even in summer,[1] — not to mention obstacles like pressure-ridges, " rubble-ice," and open lanes of water.

[1] The bears must live on seals, and seals must live on fish, and there are no fish in deep oceans so far from land, — certainly none in such an ocean.

The Fram is a grand ship for the purpose for which she was built, — to drift beset in the polar pack; and in that unprecedented three years' drift she endured every kind and degree of pressure that such ice as she encountered could exert. Yet it is by no means certain — in fact it is quite improbable — that the Fram could withstand the pressure of the paleocrystic ice, or even of the heavy pack-ice, twenty feet thick on the average, that Berry found north of Bering Sea.

The Fram was lying in open water, moored to a floe, when frozen in, and surrounded by a few large floes of "tolerably thick ice," as Nansen describes it. This ice had probably formed on the sea, one hundred to two hundred miles to the southward, the preceding winter, and had drifted north. So the ship remained, during her whole drift, in the midst of a very extensive field of new ice mixed with

year-old ice, which had grown to be three
and four years old before she got free.
Yet the unbroken floes were only seven
or eight feet thick, and such was the ice
that repeatedly over-rode the floe in which
the Fram was frozen, and that was broken
up against her side or split against her
wedge-shaped stern. No one who has
seen the paleocrystic ice will believe that
any ship could live in it for long, and a
ship, once in it, might have to live in it
for many years. (To be pushed far up
an inclined plane on the first encounter
would be her only salvation.) But there
is no question of anybody voluntarily entering the paleocrystic ice. Yet Nansen
speaks in this way of the old ice seen on
his poleward journey : —

"Sometimes it happened that we passed
through places where the ice was 'un-
usually massive, with high hummocks, so
that it looked like undulating country

covered with snow.' This was undoubtedly very old ice, which had drifted in the
polar sea for a long time on its way from
the Siberian Sea [?] to the east coast of
Greenland, and which had been subjected
year after year to severe pressure. High
hummocks and mounds are thus formed,
which summer after summer are partially
melted by the rays of the sun, and again
in the winters covered with great drifts
of snow, so that they assume forms which
resemble ice-hills rather than piles of sea
ice resulting from upheaval."[1]   (This
was in latitude 85.°)

When in latitude 86° he writes in his
diary: "I will go on one day longer, however, to see if the ice is really as bad farther northward as it appears to be from
the ridge, thirty feet in height, where we
are encamped. We hardly made four
miles yesterday. Lanes, ridges, and end-

[1] Vol. ii., pp. 140, 141, *Farthest North.*

less rough ice, it looks like an endless moraine of ice-blocks; and this continual lifting of the sledges over every irregularity is enough to tire out giants. Curious, this rubble-ice. For the most part it is not so very massive, and seems as if it had been forced up somewhat recently, for it is incompletely covered with thin, loose snow, through which one falls suddenly up to one's middle. And thus it extends mile after mile northward, while every now and then there are old floes, with mounds that have been rounded off by the action of the sun in the summer, — often very massive ice." [1]

Again — in contrast to the above — on the homeward journey, Nansen says : " The ice we are now stopping in seems to me to be something like that we had around the Fram. We have about got down to the region where she is drift-

[1] Vol. ii., pp. 167, 168, *Farthest North.*

ing."[1] He easily recognizes the difference.

Again he sums up, as follows : "The ridges were fairly high in some places, and reached a height of twenty-five feet or so. I had a good opportunity here of observing how they assume forms like ice-mountains,[2] with high, straight sides, caused by the splitting of old ridges transversely in several directions. I have often on this journey seen massive high hummocks with similar square sides, and of great circumference, sometimes quite resembling snow-covered islands. They are of 'paleocrystic ice,' as good as any one can wish."[3] Nansen adds that no real icebergs were ever seen by him nor by the men on the Fram during this expedition — nothing but sea ice.

---

[1] Vol. ii., p. 179, *Farthest North.*
[2] Icebergs, of inland fresh-water glacier ice.
[3] Vol. ii., p. 184, *Farthest North.*

Yet, in spite of the ice conditions that Nansen found the farther he traveled north, he suggests a future drifting expedition " through Bering Strait and thence northward."

No doubt if the season proved favorable and if the ship could get as far north as Lieutenant Berry did in the Rodgers, — one hundred and fifty miles northeasterly from where the Jeannette was frozen in, — the drift would be across the Pole, or very near it. I feel forced to conclude, however, from Nansen's description of the ice in the region towards the Pole, and from the formidable character and evident age of the ice towards the Greenland side of the current which passes Spitzbergen, some 100 miles to the westward of the line in which the Fram would have drifted if she had not got free — ice which even a Scoresby could never penetrate — that, possibly, it might take

ten years for a ship to drift directly
across the Pole from north of Bering Sea.
For, indeed, it is across the Pole probably, and between the Pole and Greenland, that the paleocrystic ice slowly and
gradually works out into the East Greenland stream, and consequently this drift
may not be half so rapid as that by the
route of the Jeannette and the Fram.

I can hardly believe that any conceivable vessel could "stand the racket" in
such heavy ice for that length of time.[1]
For even the Fram got strained so that
she leaked badly in three years of ice-
pressure — not so very much worse than
that of the middle-pack of Baffin's Bay.
While, if the ship were crushed halfway
across, no news of her discoveries could
ever transpire.

Dr. Nansen believes in deep water at

[1] See Payer's *New Lands within the Arctic Circle*,
and De Long's *Voyage of the Jeannette.*

the Pole. His drift gives new data in
favor of that theory, for he says: " For
various reasons, I am led to believe that
in a northerly direction also this deep sea
is of considerable extent. In the first
place, nothing was observed, either during the drift of the Fram or during our
sledge expedition to the north, that would
point to the proximity of any considerable
expanse of land; the ice seemed to drift
unimpeded, particularly in a northerly
direction. The way in which the drift
set straight to the north as soon as there
was a southerly wind was most striking.
It was with the greatest difficulty that
the wind could head the drift back towards the southeast. Had there been
any considerable expanse of land within
reasonable distance to the north of us,
it would have blocked the free movement
of the ice in that direction. Besides, the
large quantity of drift-ice, which drifts

southward with great rapidity along the east coast of Greenland all the way down to Cape Farewell and beyond it, seems to point in the same direction. Such extensive ice-fields must have a still larger breadth of sea to come from than that through which we drifted. Had the Fram continued her drift, instead of breaking loose to the north of Spitzbergen, she would certainly have come down along the coast of Greenland; but probably she would not have got close in to that coast, but would have had a certain quantity of ice between her and it; and that ice must come from a sea lying north of our route." [1]

It was unfortunate that Nansen was so enamored of the old theory of the shallowness of the polar basin. He says: "I presupposed a shallow polar sea," [2] and

---

[1] Vol. ii., pp. 707, 708, *Farthest North*.

[2] Vol. i., p. 368, *Farthest North*.

other references could be made. Consequently he did not provide any deep-sea
sounding apparatus, when everything else
was provided. Although enough incom-
plete soundings were taken to prove the
oceanic depth of the whole route covered
by the drift of the Fram, yet no sound-
ing-line appears ever to have reached the
bottom from July 22, 1895 (2056 fathoms), to July 8, 1896 (1841 fathoms) in
a distance of some 500 miles. The im-
provised apparatus was too clumsy, and
was always breaking. Yet, after proving
the theory of the drift, the depth of the
sea was of the next importance, and a
continuous and regular line of deep-sea
soundings all the way, with a correspond-
ing table of deep-sea temperatures, and of
specimens of the sea bottom, would have
been of paramount value for all time.

Dr. John Murray, of the Challenger,
would also have wished " to observe the

temperature of the ocean at all depths and seasons of the year ; " . . . "to sound, trawl, and dredge, and study the character and distribution of marine organisms."

The Franz Josef Land route to the Pole has been the only one left — in the minds of the leading Arctic experts — for the last sixteen years since the Jeannette Expedition. It is scarcely necessary to remark that Nansen has left Jackson nothing better to do than to direct his efforts to the eastward, and there is much valuable work yet to be done in that direction.

Jackson's plan for his expedition was only in theory when Nansen sailed, because that was before Harmsworth came forward to provide the ways and means. The nearest parallel in Arctic history to that romantic and fortunate meeting of Nansen with Jackson was when McClure, at the Bay of Mercy in 1853, who had come in from the Pacific and had not seen a stranger for three years, saw Lieutenant Pim coming alone over the ice — "this solitary helper out of the frozen deep." Everybody will remember that McClure then abandoned the Investigator, taking refuge in another of the Franklin search ships on the Atlantic side, thus completing the Northwest Passage on foot.

March 20, 1897.

PEARY'S NEW PLAN FOR REACHING THE POLE.

LIEUTENANT PEARY's latest plan is to go by ship up Smith's Sound, in the track of Hall, Nares, and Greely, and to establish a colony of "Arctic Highlanders" — men, dogs, women, and children, with all their belongings — at the entrance of the Sherard Osborn fiord, which is very near the north end of the mainland of Greenland. Thence, after establishing advance stations and depots, he expects to follow the coasts and channels of the North Greenland archipelago, which by many is supposed to extend far towards the Pole.

Although from general considerations previously stated, and especially from the

meeting of the tides in Kennedy Channel,
I do not coincide in the belief that the
Greenland archipelago extends very far
north, it is at least the nearest of known,
and probably of unknown lands to the
Pole, and any plan of Lieutenant Peary's
must claim our very serious attention.
His first plan of a cross-country route to
the Pole over the inland ice, with the aid
of dogs, was absolutely original, and his
first great trip was a tremendous success.
His second trip was elaborately planned,
and failed in its main objects only from
circumstances that could hardly have been
foreseen.   Yet on this second trip he had
many valuable, even though painful ex-
periences, which will throw a brilliant
light on the path of future sledge-expe-
ditions across glaciated continents.   For
as Livingstone pointed the way for Stanley, and De Long for Nansen, so Peary
has established the method for exploring

the Antarctic Continent and reaching the South Pole.

The navigation of Smith's Sound is exceedingly difficult, and annual supply-ships cannot be counted upon with such certainty as at Franz Josef Land, or at South Victoria Land, in the Antarctic. The Alert and Discovery made successful voyages both ways. So did the Proteus on her first trip. The Polaris was beset and destroyed on her way back; the Neptune could not reach Greely, and the Proteus was crushed on her second trip.

The Esquimaux colony could probably subsist by hunting, although not so well at Sherard Osborn fiord, and the ship might not reach so high a point; but Hall's expedition found seals and plenty of musk-oxen at Newman Bay, not quite so far up, at Thank God Harbor seals, even the large *phoca barbata*, were very abundant, and there is every reason to assume that there are musk-oxen, seals, and even occasional bears throughout the archipelago, though probably less abundant towards the extreme northern part.

The colony at the head of Robeson Channel would be the most available base from which thoroughly to explore and map out the whole North Greenland archipelago with all its channels. Then Peary might follow the course of the migrations of the Esquimaux and of the musk-oxen around to the north of the inland ice, through the Peary Channel to Independence Bay, and thence down the east coast of Greenland to Cape Bismarck, living mostly on the musk-oxen that he would be likely to find on the way, with an occasional seal or bear. He would thus accomplish the plans that he was prevented by so many accidents from carrying out on his last sledge-journey, and complete the exploration of all that

North Greenland region, a work in which
he has already borne so distinguished a
part.

Believing, however, in a deep ocean at
the Pole that must extend very far, on
the American side, towards Greenland, I
cannot but feel that the north-polar part
of Peary's scheme is impracticable. Let
us suppose that the islands should extend
to latitude 84°, and that Peary should
start from that position as well prepared
as Nansen was when he finally left the
Fram, with all the dogs his party could
manage; then he would have 360 geographical miles of the polar pack to trav-
erse, — 720 miles in all, — and he would
have the current either across his course
or partially against him from the start,
and directly against him, undoubtedly,
before he got halfway to the Pole; and
on his way back he would be in imminent
danger of being drifted out into East

Greenland seas. As to the difficulty of traveling over the polar pack, we have the testimony of Nansen and of Admiral Markham ; and we should remember that there would be little or no game to be found anywhere near the Pole on those deep seas.

Nansen got north about 130 miles, partly across but somewhat with the drift, and then went southwesterly some 360 miles, partly across, indeed, but mostly with the drift. This journey lasted through a very long Arctic season of some five and one half months, and his course led him over little such ice as Peary would be likely to meet with from the start.

Peary may not find so rapid a current in this region north of Greenland as Nansen found on the other side of the Pole, and the movement of the ice may not so seriously affect his journey as the

preceding comparison might suggest.
There are many indications that the main
stream of the polar current flows along
the general course of the drift of the
Fram, though the Jeannette relics may
have been carried over a more northern
route and at a faster rate, since they were
borne the same distance in two years as
the Fram in three. The Jeannette was
fairly in the current when the articles
were left upon the floe, but it looks as if
the Fram lost half a year before she got
well into the stream. Nansen's drift back
to the southeast for a hundred miles, after
the ship was frozen in, points to the existence of an oceanic eddy to the westward of the submarine bank on which
the New Siberian group of islands stands
— the Jeannette current passing northwesterly through the deep sea to the
north of the islands. There are similar
eddies in the Arctic seas — the Kara Sea,

and the central part of Baffin's Bay, which is occupied by the middle-pack.

Sir Wyville Thompson's theory of a current circling about the polar sea — passing into it at Nova Zembla and coming out on the east side of Greenland — would necessarily have led to the inference that the whole central part of the polar area was occupied by a broad eddy; a great Sargasso sea, which instead of being covered with floating seaweed, driftwood, and all the derelicts of the Atlantic, would have been entirely filled with ancient and massive ice — perhaps a polar ice-cap.

This speculation suggests Melville's theory [1] of an " immovable ice-cap, held in place by undiscovered islands, occupying the space within the eighty-fifth degree of latitude." Nansen's discoveries have at

---

[1] *In the Lena Delta*, by Chief Engineer George W. Melville, U. S. Navy, p. 475.

least displaced this theoretical ice-cap, and have pushed it farther over towards the American side. In that case it might not be far across from the last island north of Greenland to the edge of the ice-cap, an inference which seems to be sustained by Melville, as he says on the same page, "Having reached the firm ice-cap, which covers the earth to the north of 85°, the travel will be smooth and easy."

Although I can find no place in the polar basin for either the smooth "immovable ice-cap," or for the rough, broken and revolving ice-cap of a deep Sargasso sea, yet it seems to me now, that in the region west of Grinnell Land and halfway between the Parry Islands and the Pole the ice may have a very sluggish movement, even if there are no islands to hold it in place.

The powerful East Greenland current has a general tendency to draw all the surface water, with its icy burden, out from the polar sea towards the Atlantic. This strong suction exerts its greatest force in the direction of the polar current along to the northward of the earlier portion of the course of the Fram, although quite in the line, it may be, of Sverdrup's drift the latter part of the way. The currents flowing through the numerous channels that lead to Baffin's Bay, the northwest winds that may preponderate, and perhaps islands, constantly tend to hold down the paleocrystic ice against the North American and North Greenland coasts.

Between the respective spheres of influence of the great polar stream and of the currents leading to Baffin's Bay, there may be an area of slow and irregular drift in which the ice may have time to grow very old. I have written across the face of my polar map, from opposite the mouth of the Mackenzie to a point north-west of Grinnell Land and far towards the Pole, " THE PALEOCRYSTIC SEA."

In consideration of all the foregoing reasons, I am not sure that the movement of the ice in a southerly and easterly direction would interfere so seriously as might be supposed with Peary's projected journey, although I still think that the rough and broken character of the pack would prevent the attainment of the North Pole. Peary, like Nansen, would know when to turn back, and would in this way make a valuable contribution to geographical and hydrographical science. He might also surpass Nansen's highest latitude, and set a new mark to tempt the ambition of future explorers.

April 14, 1897.

In the Antarctic, there is everything to be done. Yet I have little to add to my "The North Pole and the South Pole" paper on this subject, except that steamers have been down there since 1890, and Borchegrevink has found not only a place to land, but even a very suitable place for a station, at Cape Adair, an especially convenient headquarters for work at the south magnetic pole — perhaps the most pressing and timely work to be done in the Antarctic, — but too far away and badly situated for an attack on the South Pole.

Admiral Nares prefers Weddell's route, and Dr. John Murray theorizes that the nearest coast to the South Pole would be

directly south of the farthest point attained by Weddell in 1823, southeastward
from Cape Horn and east of Graham's
Land. Weddell sailed to 75° S., and
Captain Larsen and other sealers have recently steamed down the east coast of
Graham's Land and found a loose pack
and much open water.

Indeed, it is probable that Ross and
Weddell, so long ago, found the two deep-
est indentations in the Antarctic land and
the two best routes for a near approach
to the Southern Pole. For it seems quite
certain that the warm tropical current
that flows south along the east coast of
South America must sink beneath the cold
Cape Horn current and have an influence
towards keeping the water open east of
Graham's Land. The prevailing westerly
winds, too, may blow the ice away from
Graham's Land and loosen up the pack.

The Australian current and the prevailing winds may have a similar influence east of Victoria Land, where Sir James Ross reached 78° S. and explored the whole coast in two successive voyages. Captain Kristensen had little difficulty in following Ross's course in 1894–95, reaching 74° S., and could easily have gone farther. No one had undertaken this voyage since Ross in 1841 and 1842, and Kristensen with his small sealing steamer Antarctic has shown how superior steamers are to sailing vessels for such work.

Dr. Murray suggests that a proper station could probably be found at Macmurdo Bay, near Mt. Erebus, and such a base would be very desirable for the exploration of the inland ice, for Ross's icy barrier, a broad, smooth glacier, level and free from crevasses, would afford good opportunity for sledge traveling, besides being the nearest known coast to the South Pole, the shortest distance. It extends so far inland towards the south that no land, no mountains, no high inland-ice horizon can be seen behind it (Ben Nevis could not have been seen from Geikie's ice-cliff), and it would probably take a man a long way towards the Pole before reaching any high altitude. It would be only some seven hundred miles to the Pole, about the distance Peary went over the inland ice to the northeasterly end of Greenland at Independence Bay.

The success of Peary's journeys, however, depended upon the use of Esquimaux dogs; and whether Arctic dogs would live to be carried across the equator on shipboard is not known. If a few out of many should live, large numbers could be bred from such a stock on some Antarctic island.

But even Peary's dogs froze to death on his second journey across the inland ice of Northern Greenland, and the blizzards would be still worse, perhaps, on the probably high glaciated continent of the Antarctic, which is supposed to be still colder than the Arctic.

Then Peary, at the end of his terrible journey to Independence Bay, found the musk-ox, and on both trips men and dogs took a vacation and recuperated, getting new life and strength for dogs and men — as dogs on such a trip are equal to men, and more useful than men; for when they break down there is no moral objection to their being killed and eaten by the men or by the other dogs, which is quite as advantageous.

As far as I can learn, Peary would never have been able to get back across the inland ice if he had not had the good fortune to lay in a new stock of energy for men and dogs in the shape of musk-ox meat.[1]

[1] See Appendix, *The East Greenland Musk-Ox.*

Dogs had never been used on inland ice when I wrote my "Overland" paper in 1889, and I remember figuring out an elaborate plan of a grand campaign on the Franklin-search system of supporting man-sledges, to establish a scientific station at the South Pole, — an ambitious project, and perhaps impracticable. It is evident that Peary's remarkably successful work in Greenland must be the basis for similar undertakings in the exploration of the Antarctic Continent, and the plan of his last journey, improved and corrected from his experience, must be used in any serious attempt to get to the South Pole.

Peary's advanced depot, upon which the success of his whole trip depended, was drifted over and rendered unfindable; and it is plain that the future explorer of inland ice will have to flag his whole course as far as stations are established and depots are laid down, just as the teamsters bush their roads across the northern lakes. A line of large bamboo poles could perhaps be deeply and firmly set, with small and durable flags or aluminum vanes at the top. Very likely many of them would be buried in the snow-drifts, and some might be blown down or broken off, but not all of them, and such a line could be followed if the poles were not set too far apart.

Then with a considerable force of men to lay out the preliminary stations and depots, and with great packs of dogs — that it would take years to breed — and a system of supporting sledges, the final party of a few men with many dogs could be sent off to complete the journey to the Pole.

But it would be a mistake to start too early in the spring, for the blizzards in which many of the dogs would freeze to death would be less likely to occur later in the season. I fear there will have to be much painful experience before the South Pole is attained. Still, it is possible of attainment, which can hardly be said with certainty of the North Pole, even though Nansen got so near it, and has shown us the only way to get there, with his drifting ship and his original system of traveling over the polar pack with dogs and kayak-sledges.

March 13, 1897.

[1] For a full understanding of the whole Antarctic question, see Dr. John Murray's remarkable paper (and map), "The Renewal of Antarctic Exploration," in *The Geographical Journal* (Royal Geographical Society) of January, 1894, with the " discussion " following the reading of the paper.

APPENDIX

I

21 ECCLESTON SQUARE, S. W., LONDON,
18 December, 1881.

MY DEAR SIR, — I beg to acknowledge the receipt of your letter, dated November 25th, inclosing a paper on Arctic research, and of your second letter dated December 1st. I have read your paper with much interest, and perceive that it is the result of extensive reading and much thought. It is both gratifying and interesting to find that Arctic questions are studied with so much care. I therefore regret the more that, owing to the author not having been personally engaged on Arctic service, it is not considered to be adapted for publication in the Proceedings of the Royal Geographical Society.

I agree with you that a search down the

Mackenzie would be fruitless.   My opinion is that De Long shaped a course westward and northward, and that if the Jeannette ever reached a harbor, it was on an unknown shore to the north of Siberia.   I saw Mr. Gordon Bennett to-day, and he assures me that De Long was instructed to endeavor to meet Nordenskjöld before proceeding on his own discoveries.   Consequently he must certainly have gone westward.

On the 20th I shall accompany Lord Aberdare, with a Deputation, to urge upon the First Lord of the Admiralty the urgent necessity for sending a steamer to relieve Mr. Leigh Smith, and consequently to visit Franz Josef Land next season.   I trust that we may be successful, but it is by no means certain.

I only wish that we could persuade our Government to undertake an adequate exploration of Franz Josef Land, and to send another steamer to search for the Jeannette. But I regret to say that I see very little hope of it.   My very strong opinion, and in this I concur with Lieutenant Hovgaard, is that a search ought to be undertaken to Cape Chelyuskin, and northwards on or near the meridian of that cape. I hope that Hovgaard, who has gone to America to collect funds, may be successful, and that if he goes to Cape Chelyuskin, Lieutenant Schwatka may accompany him, to conduct the sledging work.

I believe that you are right in supposing that the drift along the south shore of Franz Josef Land is from east to west; but there is nothing but mere conjecture to indicate the direction of currents north of Siberia. . . .

Ever, yours very truly,

CLEMENTS R. MARKHAM.

HENRY M. PRENTISS, ESQ.,
    Bangor, Maine, United States.

II

THE HERALD, NEW YORK,
November 14, 1883.

DEAR SIR, — We have carefully considered your communication, dated November 6. While we are flattered by the views you so kindly take, we are unable to publish the matter. In view of all the facts that have been presented concerning the unfortunate expedition, we scarcely need explain to you that it would be inappropriate for the Herald to publish it. Of course, any other journal in the country could better afford to do it, in view of our relations to the expedition, than the Herald. From this you will probably understand the feeling which prompts us to return you the MS., in case you desire to use it elsewhere.

Remaining very truly yours,

J. G. BENNETT.

H. M. PRENTISS, ESQ.,
Bangor, Maine.

III

SIR CLEMENTS MARKHAM, in his The
Threshold of the Unknown Region, pages
308–11, says that Clavering in 1823 found
twelve natives at Cape Borlase Warren, in
seventy-five degrees north, on the east coast
of Greenland; but Captain Koldewy did not
find any Esquimaux about there in 1869,
though there were abundant traces of them.
" As the Melville Bay glaciers form an impas-
sable barrier, preventing the ' Arctic Highlanders' from wandering southward on the
west side, so the ice-bound coast on the east
side would prevent the people seen by Clavering from taking a southerly course; " and
again, Markham theorizes, " These considerations lead to the conclusion that there are, or
have been, inhabitants in the unexplored region

to the north of the known parts of Greenland."
Yet skeptics may well have thought this utter-
ance a trifle far-fetched in 1873, before the
discoveries of Nares and of Greely in Grinnell
Land.

But even if Koldewy did not find the men,
he found whole herds of musk-oxen in the
same region. Now since Peary has found the
musk-ox at Independence Bay, and has thus
established the connecting link in the chain of
evidence, we find that Markham's theory is
proven, that the men as well as the musk-oxen
could and must have come around the north
end of Greenland from Smith Sound; the
course of the previous migration from the
American continent having been either up
Smith Sound or by the west coast of Grinnell
Land, across to Lady Franklin Bay, where
the musk-ox is abundant, and where there
are numerous old traces of the Esquimaux,
and across the sound to Newman Bay, where
Hall found the musk-ox and killed a great
many. Thence the Esquimaux as well as the

musk-oxen must have passed around the northerly limit of the inland ice of Greenland, explored by Peary, to Independence Bay, and
thence southerly along the east coast of Greenland to the region where Clavering and Kol-
dewey found them. So much for polar theories when based on facts and common sense.
Nansen has just proved another — and the
most important yet.